**DATE DUE**

| | | |
|---|---|---|
| MAY 1 5 1991 | | |
| | NOV 1 5 1993 | |
| SEP 2 6 1991 | APR 1 1 1994 | |
| NOV 1 1991 | | |
| JAN 2 2 1992 | JUN 2 5 1994 | |
| MAR 1 2 1992 | APR 1 9 1995 | |
| JUN 2 9 1992 | SEP 2 1 1995 | |
| JUL 2 9 1992 | AUG 1 4 1996 | |
| SEP 1 1 1992 | NOV 0 5 2016 | |
| FEB 3 1993 | | |
| MAY 1 2 1993 | | |
| JUN 0 5 1993 | | |
| SEP 0 1 1993 | | |

Bantam Books in the Choose Your Own Adventure® series
Ask your bookseller for the books you have missed

#1 THE CAVE OF TIME
#2 JOURNEY UNDER THE SEA
#3 DANGER IN THE DESERT
#4 SPACE AND BEYOND
#5 THE CURSE OF THE
  HAUNTED MANSION
#6 SPY TRAP
#7 MESSAGE FROM SPACE
#8 DEADWOOD CITY
#9 WHO KILLED HARLOWE
  THROMBEY?
#10 THE LOST JEWELS
#22 SPACE PATROL
#31 VAMPIRE EXPRESS
#52 GHOST HUNTER
#53 THE CASE OF THE SILK KING
#66 SECRET OF THE NINJA
#71 SPACE VAMPIRE
#78 RETURN TO ATLANTIS
#80 THE PERFECT PLANET
#82 HURRICANE!
#83 TRACK OF THE BEAR
#84 YOU ARE A MONSTER
#85 INCA GOLD
#86 KNIGHTS OF THE ROUND TABLE
#88 MASTER OF KUNG FU
#89 SOUTH POLE SABOTAGE

#90 MUTINY IN SPACE
#91 YOU ARE A SUPERSTAR
#92 RETURN OF THE NINJA
#93 CAPTIVE!
#94 BLOOD ON THE HANDLE
#95 YOU ARE A GENIUS
#96 STOCK CAR CHAMPION
#97 THROUGH THE BLACK HOLE
#98 YOU ARE A MILLIONAIRE
#99 REVENGE OF THE RUSSIAN
  GHOST
#100 THE WORST DAY OF YOUR LIFE
#101 ALIEN, GO HOME!
#102 MASTER OF TAE KWON DO
#103 GRAVE ROBBERS
#104 THE COBRA CONNECTION
#105 THE TREASURE OF THE
  ONYX DRAGON
#106 HIJACKED!
#107 FIGHT FOR FREEDOM
#108 MASTER OF KARATE
#109 CHINESE DRAGONS
#110 INVADERS FROM WITHIN
#111 SMOKE JUMPER
#112 SKATEBOARD CHAMPION
#113 THE LOST NINJA

#1 JOURNEY TO THE YEAR 3000 (A Choose Your Own Adventure Super Adventure)
#2 DANGER ZONES (A Choose Your Own Adventure Super Adventure)

# THE LOST NINJA

## BY JAY LEIBOLD

## ILLUSTRATED BY FRANK BOLLE

*An R.A. Montgomery Book*

**BANTAM BOOKS**
NEW YORK · TORONTO · LONDON · SYDNEY · AUCKLAND

RL 4, age 10 and up

THE LOST NINJA

*A Bantam Book / May 1991*

*CHOOSE YOUR OWN ADVENTURE® is a registered trademark of
Bantam Books, a division of Bantam Doubleday Dell Publishing
Group, Inc. Registered in U.S. Patent and Trademark Office
and elsewhere.*

*Original conception of Edward Parkard*

*Cover art by Romas Kukalis*

*Interior illustrations by Frank Bolle*

ISBN 0-553-28960-8

*Published simultaneously in the United States and Canada*

*Bantam Books are published by Bantam Books, a division of Bantam Double-
day Dell Publishing Group, Inc. Its trademark, consisting of the words
"Bantam Books" and the portrayal of a rooster, is Registered in U.S. Patent
and Trademark Office and in other countries. Marca Registrada. Bantam
Books, 666 Fifth Avenue, New York, New York 10103.*

PRINTED IN THE UNITED STATES OF AMERICA

OPM          0 9 8 7 6 5 4 3 2 1

# THE LOST NINJA

# WARNING!!!

Do not read this book straight through from beginning to end. These pages contain many different adventures that you may have as you decide whether or not to help a mysterious boy named Saito. From time to time as you read along, you will be asked to make a choice. Your choice will determine whether you are successful in saving Saito—and yourself—or whether you meet with disaster!

The adventures you have are the results of your choices. You are responsible for your fate because you make the decisions. After you make a choice, follow the instructions to find out what happens next.

Be careful! Saito may not be who he appears to be. As you find yourself involved in the dangerous world of Japanese gangsters, known as the *yakuza*, you may have to use your *ninja* powers. To find out more about *ninjutsu* and some of the other Japanese and martial arts terms in this book, read the Special Note and Glossary on the following pages.

Good luck!

# SPECIAL NOTE ON THE NINJA

The ancient art practiced by the ninja is called *ninjutsu*—the way of stealth or invisibility. In the eleventh and twelfth centuries, Japanese mountain clans drew on their knowledge of martial arts, war tactics, and mystical wisdom to develop their skills. Through the *ryu* (tradition or school), the clans secretly passed down their style from one generation to the next.

A ninja has many different skills. Each ryu has its own mix of techniques, taught by the *sensei* (teacher or master) at the *dojo* (the place where martial arts are practiced). A student of ninjutsu will learn empty-hand combat, the use of weapons and special devices, and techniques of stealth, deception, and invisibility.

The most important aspect of the martial arts is the discipline of daily practice. A student will start with basic exercises in movement and meditation and practice them until they are part of his or her everyday life. After many years of training, the student may be able to "forget" the basics and achieve a state of emptiness, which is also a state of complete awareness and readiness.

Some ninja use their powers to guide them on a path of physical and spiritual development. Others use their skills to gain power over other people. Some ninja even hire themselves out as mercenaries or assassins. Each individual must decide how he or she will use the ninja knowledge. Because this knowledge can be so potent, the consequences of its misuse may be grave.

# GLOSSARY

**Aikido**—*Ai*, harmony; *ki*, energy; *do*, the way. A defensive discipline using pivoting motions and the momentum of the attacker to neutralize the attack.

**Bujutsu**—Broad term for all Japanese warrior arts.

**Dojo**—The place where martial arts are practiced.

**Futon**—A thick, quilted mattress.

**Gaijin**—Japanese term for foreigner.

**Giri**—Obligation, duty, or loyalty expected of a member of an organization or society.

**Kaginawa**—A grapple or hook attached to the end of a rope.

**Karate**—Literally, "empty-handed." A martial art originating in Japan utilizing punches and kicks.

**Karaoke**—Literally, "empty orchestra." A bar or club where patrons get up on stage and sing along with pop songs.

**Kata**—A prearranged sequence of blocks and attacks against multiple imaginary opponents, practiced repeatedly to develop the skills of the martial arts.

**Kusari-fundo**—Ninja weapon; a length of chain with weights at either end.

**Metsubishi**—Ninja blinding powder, used to temporarily cloud the vision of an opponent.

**Ninja**—A person adept at the art of ninjutsu.

**Ninjutsu**—The "art of stealth" or "way of invisibility." An unconventional discipline incorporating martial arts, special weapons, techniques of concealment, and sorcery.

Oya-bun—Yakuza boss.

Pai Gow—Chinese game played with domino-like tiles, resembling a mixture of poker and blackjack.

Ryu—School or tradition of martial arts.

Sensei—Master, teacher.

Seppuku—Ritual suicide, an honorable form of death for samurai.

Shuriken—A metal throwing blade, often star-shaped.

Yakuza—Japanese gangsters. Once limited to Japan, they now operate all over the world.

Yubitsume—Yakuza initiation ritual in which the new member cuts off the tip of his finger to prove his loyalty.

You slam the phone down in frustration—you still can't get through to Japan. It's the third time you've tried to call your friend Nada, but the call won't go through. Sometimes you get a busy signal, sometimes you get a recording, and sometimes nothing at all.

You're at your family's house in Oakland, California after living in Japan for almost two years. Looking back, it seems more like ten. Originally, you went to study *karate* and Japanese culture. But everything changed very quickly when you met Nada Kurayama. She introduced you to a new discipline called *aikido* at her family *dojo*. It did not take long for the two of you to become fast friends.

You became much more involved with the Kurayama family when they received a mysterious sword in the mail. It brought dangerous disruptions to the dojo. Together you and Nada solved the mystery of the sword. Along the way, you discovered a stunning secret about the Kurayama: they were a *ninja* family, going back hundreds of years.

Nada had given up *ninjutsu* for a time because she feared its power. But after solving the mystery of the sword, she started practicing again. You began to learn the art of the ninja as well. Eventually Nada took over the family dojo, and you became an instructor. When one of your students was kidnapped, you had to draw on all your ninja powers to get him back safely.

*Turn to page 2.*

**2**

On your flight back to the U.S., you reflected that, all in all, it had been an amazing two years. You were now more versed in the martial arts than you ever could have expected. And, more importantly than becoming a strong fighter, you had discovered a spiritual side to your discipline.

Returning home, you felt like a very different person than when you left. It was not easy to come back. You were glad to see your family, but you missed Nada and the dojo. You decided to finish your education first, then, if you still wanted to, return to Japan.

At first it was hard readjusting to life back in the States. You had become used to the tightly packed spaces and orderliness of Japan. Back home it seemed as if there was too much space and everything was chaotic. You'd also grown to enjoy being a foreigner, an object of curiosity, there. Here in Oakland, you're just another face in the melting pot.

Another thing you miss is the discipline of martial arts study. You came to value the early morning stretching exercises, the endless repetition of *kata*, prearranged fight sequences, and the time set aside for meditation. In Japan it was accepted as normal practice; here in the U.S. it is more of a novelty. You have to make a point of sticking to your discipline, which your friends find hard to understand.

*Go on to the next page.*

You're now enrolled in a dojo in the section of San Francisco known as Japantown. Every afternoon you take the BART train to the dojo for aikido instruction. You don't want to lose your edge, but it's hard—there are so many distractions in American life.

Some days after class you linger in Japantown, savoring the flavor of the surroundings. You almost feel like you're back in Japan. Often you go to the Haiku Tea Room for a cup of green tea. You love to watch as the tea is prepared in the traditional way.

It was here, three days ago, that you had your first encounter with a boy named Saito, whom you had noticed in your aikido class.

When Saito approached, the hairs stood up on the back of your neck. You had no idea why. You recall the first time you had seen him. You were sure you'd never met him before, yet he looked so familiar it was eerie. Unconsciously you've been avoiding him.

Saito came into the tearoom and sat beside you without asking, without a word of greeting. This did not surprise you. You'd noticed in class that he was very aggressive. He seemed to take too much pleasure in putting an opponent on the mat. This is not your style at all. You prefer to think of sparring as a kind of dance where aggression is just one of the steps. You see yourself and your opponent as part of the same flow of energy. "You can turn a hit into a gift," the *sensei,* your master teacher, liked to say. But Saito seemed to enjoy aggression for its own sake. He seemed to have something to prove.

*Turn to page 46*.

**4**

A little way across the bridge something suddenly jerks on your leg. You and Saito are thrust against the door as if some incredible force were trying to pull you out of the car. The pull on your leg increases, and you scream in pain.

The same invisible force seems to take control of the wheel, jerking the car to the right, causing it to bounce against the curb a few times before the driver jams on the brakes. As soon as he does, the car is dragged backward several feet, slightly relieving the stress on your leg.

"The bungy cords!" you cry. "We forgot to take them off."

"I told you they were strong," Saito says, grimacing as he tries to release his ankle.

"What the devil!?" the detective exclaims, glaring back at you.

"Keep backing up," Saito tells the driver.

*Turn to page 21.*

"Dive!" you yell, plunging into the water. Saito splashes in beside you, and together you swim as far as you can underwater. When you surface, bullets are zinging into the water all around you. You see a small sailboat tied up nearby, and so does Saito.

The two of you swim for the boat and quickly pull yourselves over the gunwale. Splintered wood flies as bullets ricochet off the hull. Keeping low, you untie the boat and push away from the dock. Saito raises the sail. As usual, there is a strong breeze on the bay, and you zoom away.

The sail is full of bullet holes, but it still catches the wind. Once you're out of range, you look back to see the yakuza untying their boat and backing away from the dock. It's a much larger craft, though, and is slow to get away.

*Turn to page 10.*

But something about Saito haunted you. You finally decided this afternoon to call Nada. Normally you keep in touch by mail, but you felt the need to talk to her in person.

Now you slam down the phone in frustration. You can't get through. Looking at your watch, you realize it's time for you to leave for the dojo.

During class you feel Saito's eyes on you, but he doesn't say anything. Afterward you go to the tearoom as usual, looking forward to its warmth and comfort.

You're not surprised when Saito shows up. He appears to have decided you like his company. Your feelings about this are mixed. You're flattered by the attention. There's something intriguing about him, and he's certainly skilled in the martial arts.

On the other hand, you dislike his childish, sometimes abrasive manner. You feel that he's both criticizing and trying to impress you at the same time.

Though he can't be much more than twenty years old, his face has a worn look, as if he's been through a lot. As he sits down, Saito points to a pair of men drinking tea across the room. "Watch that man lift his cup. See how he's missing part of a finger? He's a *yakuza*—a gangster. They cut off the first joint of their small finger as a sign of loyalty to their boss. It's called *yubitsume*. If they make a mistake, the boss will cut off the rest of the finger."

*Turn to page 51.*

**8**

The door clicks shut behind Minoru. You hear a bolt being locked. Now you're sure that something very bad is happening. Minoru sees you as a commodity. You don't want to think about what kind of commodity. The point is, you need to get out.

The more you think about Minoru's words and his smug, slimy manner, the madder you get. How dare he do this to you? First he spikes your drink, then he locks you up in this cubicle. Now he's planning to take you across the ocean like a piece of merchandise and sell you in some kind of market.

Your blood boils. You want to kick down the walls. Testing them out, you can tell they're pretty flimsy—just some plaster and wood. You could destroy them with a few kicks. You're tempted to do it. If nothing else, it will teach Minoru a lesson.

*If you decide to kick through the walls, turn to page 62.*

*If you decide not to demonstrate your power just yet, turn to page 49.*

The screeching sound of tires makes you look up. Something bizarre is happening outside.

A black car has stopped in front of Saito. His face shows immediate panic. Before he can move, two men jump out. One grabs him by the collar of his jacket. They struggle for a moment, tearing the lining. Saito tries to throw the man, but the man knows how to counter the move. He pins Saito's arms behind his back, and the other man delivers a brutal punch to his stomach. Saito doubles over in pain.

You jump from your seat as the men shove him into the car. By the time you're out the door, the car has sped off. Bystanders are staring after it, confused. "Did anyone get the license plate number?" you ask. But everyone just shakes their heads.

You look down at the spot where the struggle occurred. A piece of paper has fallen out of Saito's jacket. You stuff it in your pocket and look for the nearest telephone to report the incident to the police.

*Turn to page 52.*

## 10

Saito is at the rudder. The boat is tacking wildly. You jump back and forth from port to starboard as it shifts direction. "You're doing a great job," you assure Saito.

He laughs. "I've never done this before in my life."

Suddenly a big tanker looms ahead. You motion Saito to cut in front of it. A horn bellows from the tanker, but you just make it. You turn and watch the enormous prow of the ship go by overhead.

You try to relax a little—the tanker is hiding you from the yakuza boat. If you can keep the big ship between the two of you, you may be able to escape.

Suddenly you notice that there are several inches of water in the boat. The bullets have turned it into a sieve!

Saito notices it, too. "I hope you're a good swimmer," you say.

*Turn to page 112.*

It's everything you can do to keep yourself from opening your eyes as footsteps approach the van. What's Saito doing here? you wonder.

You decide to find out sooner rather than later. Saito is taking away the first box. You prick up your ears, listening for sounds of anyone else nearby. The coast seems clear.

"Psst! Saito!" you hiss when he comes back.

"Huh?" he says, surprised. He steps up into the van and lets out a gasp. "What—what are you doing here?"

"I was going to ask you the same thing. I'm not here by choice."

Saito is about to reply when a voice commands, "Saito, get the forklift!"

"Forget the forklift," you hiss. "Get me out of here."

"I can't," he says, starting to leave.

"At least untie me," you insist.

Saito climbs over the boxes and hurriedly works at your knots. "I'm taking a big risk," he mutters.

Once he has left, you get your hands and legs free of your bonds. You know someone will come for you soon. Maybe the boxes will help you. You tear one open and step back, frightened by what you find inside—it's packed full of handguns, all made of gleaming black steel.

The whining engine of the forklift approaches. You're not sure what Saito's intentions are, but now is a good time to put him to the test.

*Turn to page 54.*

Is Saito involved with the yakuza? you wonder. And if he is, what should you do about it? You look once again at the address on the napkin. Sumioto's is in a dangerous part of the city. Not only that, you know it's a bad idea to cross the yakuza. If it turns out Saito is mixed up with them, it's his problem. Why should you put your head on the line for some obnoxious guy you barely know?

Yet you can't escape the strange sense of familiarity about Saito. You have an inexplicable urge to help him. You're curious about his connection to the Kurayama family. And you wonder if in his own way Saito has been asking you for help this past week, even though he was unable to come right out and say so.

You wish you could talk to Nada, but you can't right now. You're going to have to decide by yourself whether to look into Saito's disappearance or not. Sumioto's would be the logical place to start. But perhaps you should turn the napkin over to the police in the morning and let them handle it.

---

*If you decide to try and help Saito,*
*turn to page 56.*

*If you decide to let the police handle it,*
*turn to page 81.*

Frustrated, you go back outside. Maybe there's another entrance. Squeezing through a dark walkway between buildings, you circle around to the back when suddenly you have a strange feeling— you whirl around and face a man who has been following you. "The back door is locked," he says in a voice he probably thinks is suave. You can't make out his face in the dark, but you imagine he has a sinister smile. You go into a defensive mode, ready for anything.

"So, young one, you want to sing in the karaoke." Karaoke means "empty orchestra." A karaoke bar plays popular music videos while the patrons take turns getting up on stage and singing the songs.

"No," you answer bluntly.

"Ah, but I can tell that you do. Please allow me to be your escort. I will see to it that the hostess lets you in."

*Turn to page 34.*

You relate some of your conversation from the night before. "Saito was willing to give up his life," you say.

A little smile plays across Wujan's lips. "The moment you have given up is the moment you are ready to begin," he says. "Saito, if you like, you may stay here. You will be safe from the yakuza. You will be my student."

Saito bows his head. "I am honored, sensei. I would like to stay."

"Good," Wujan says. He shuffles over to a corner and brings Saito a broom. "You can start by sweeping out the dojo."

As Saito leaves the room, Wujan gives you a complicit smile. "Keep him on his toes," you say.

Wujan gives you a ride down to a bus station. You're glad Saito's safe. However, you never did figure out what was so familiar-looking about him.

**The End**

You whirl to see the captain with the first mate, each holding a pistol. You put up your hands, hoping Debbie will arrive soon. She does, poking her head out the hatchway behind the captain. "Hold it!" she says, taking aim with her pistol.

"Go ahead and shoot," the captain snarls, advancing on you.

Debbie holds her breath and pulls the trigger. Nothing happens—the safety is on. The first mate runs up and grabs the gun from her. "Everyone back down!" he commands, herding Debbie and the rest of the kids back into their prison.

The captain keeps his gun trained on you. As the other two crew members get to their feet, he orders them to bring some chains. "Minoru was right," he says to you. "There's always one bad apple in the bunch. And there's only one thing you can do with it—toss it out."

As the crew wraps you up in chains, you realize that the captain is not using a figure of speech.

**The End**

## 18

When you wake up, you find that you're in a small cubicle. There is a *futon* mattress on the floor, a glass of water next to it, and four white walls. The door to the room is small but made of metal. You try the handle. The door does not budge a millimeter.

You lie back down on the futon and try to think, but you become drowsy again and drift away.

The next time you wake up, you're being shaken by Minoru. A broad smile is on his face. He holds a plate of fish and rice. "Time to eat," he says, offering the food.

You just glare at him. "What's going on here? I want to leave."

Minoru gives you another one of his syrupy smiles. "We will leave soon," he assures you. "We will travel the sea. A new world awaits you."

"What are you talking about?" you demand.

"I will take you to an exotic place," Minoru says in a smooth tone. "You will have many new friends. All your needs will be taken care of."

You don't like the sound of this at all. Once again you demand to know what is going on.

Minoru goes to the door. "You will find out soon enough," he says. "Let's just say you'll be helping out your country's trade deficit."

*Turn to page 8.*

## 20

"Can I get you anything?" Suddenly you realize the question is directed at you. You look up to see the waitress poised to take your order.

"No," you reply, shaking your head emphatically. She gives you an odd look and starts to move away. You realize her look is one of sympathy.

"Wait—yes!" you say, motioning her back. You cup your hand to the side of your mouth. She leans down to hear. Quietly, in Japanese, you describe Saito and ask if she knows him.

"Oh yes," she whispers back to you. "He works here as a bouncer some nights. But I haven't seen him tonight."

You dig in your pocket and pull out a hefty tip. "Would you mind trying to find out if anyone knows where he is—discreetly?"

With a quick glance to either side, she pockets the tip, nods, and moves on to the next table. You sit back and survey the room, wondering if anyone was watching. Minoru is still in back, apparently engaged in conversation with the bartender.

*Turn to page 82.*

Once you've gotten yourselves untied from the bungy cords, Saito explains his plan. "What a couple of idiots!" the detective explodes. "At the very best, you're going to be charged with malicious mischief and destroying police property—if we don't get you for arson."

A few minutes later, the detective looks back at you and says in a quiet voice, "You'd better have the goods on Hideomi."

As it turns out, Saito does. He produces enough evidence to put Hideomi and his men away. All charges against you are dismissed. You're both put in the witness protection program to keep you safe from the yakuza. One of these days, the welt on your ankle will heal. And one of these days, you'll go back to Japan with Saito to help him reconcile with Nada and his family. But for now you're just glad you didn't have to make that jump.

**The End**

You go outside with Saito to his motor scooter. "Wait a minute," you say. "I thought you were taking the bus."

Saito grins. "Just trying to avoid you."

You shake your head and smile, then hop on the back of the scooter. Saito loans you his helmet for the ride over to Happy Boy, his favorite diner.

As you eat, Saito tells you his story—at least most of it. You have a feeling he's leaving something out.

Saito grew up in Japan, he tells you, where his family ran a karate dojo. He was an excellent student and advanced very quickly. From an early age he was in line to become the sensei of the dojo. But something happened. Trying to make money outside the dojo, he fell into disgrace and dishonored his family. Fed up with Japanese tradition, he came to the United States to start over.

But somewhere along the way he lost his original purpose. He had no problem finding work teaching karate, but before long he got bored. He started staying out late at nightclubs and gambling dens. He got hooked on Pai Gow, a Chinese game similar to poker and blackjack.

With his keen sense of perception, he was able to win money at Pai Gow. But as he left behind his martial arts discipline and lived the fast life, he lost his touch. He began to lose. He played more, only to lose more.

*Turn to page 86.*

"So you're just going to go along with this?" you ask.

"No," Saito says quietly. "I'm going to nail these guys somehow."

"Can't you just go somewhere else?"

Saito shakes his head. "They'd find me. The only way I could escape this is if I could escape my skin. Now there's an idea—plastic surgery." He bursts out laughing.

"What's so funny?" you say.

"Where would I get the money for plastic surgery?" he says, still laughing.

Suddenly you realize how serious he is. Saito notices the look on your face and says, "It's stupid to be telling you all this. What can you do? You're just a kid."

"I'll do whatever I can," you hear yourself say.

"I don't want you mixed up in this," he replies firmly. This is a side of Saito you haven't seen— concern for another. "It may not happen tomorrow night, but sooner or later I'll help nab these guys. My days will be numbered when I do, but I'd rather die that way than spend my life as a yakuza."

*Go on to the next page.*

There must be another way, you think. Desperately you try to come up with a plan. You see an image of Nada's dojo in Japan. Surely Saito would be safe there, if only you could convince him to go with you.

But he seems determined to live out his fate. Maybe you should try to come up with a plan to trap the yakuza. At least that would buy you some time—an extra day at the very least.

*If you try to convince Saito to leave town, turn to page 109.*

*If you try to come up with a plan to trap the yakuza, turn to page 89.*

For some reason you suddenly don't mind the idea of getting up to sing, in spite of the prodding you've been receiving.

You go to the front of the stage, and the DJ hands you a microphone. "What song?" he asks in Japanese.

"Anything," you say.

He cues up a Japanese pop song from last year. You know it well, though you don't especially like it. The lyrics are displayed on the video monitor, and a little green ball bounces on top of each word as it's time to sing it. You keep one eye on the monitor and the other on the crowd.

After a few lines, no one pays much attention to you. You guess they either expected you to fall on your face or they're disappointed your voice isn't better. As you go through the motions, you're able to relax and observe the goings-on in the bar.

The first thing you notice is that Minoru has an unusual interest in your drink. He's looking at it as if it might explode.

Next you see your waitress coming from the bar with a tray full of drinks. You give her a hard look, asking your question silently. She jerks her head ever so slightly upward and to the back.

You receive polite applause when the song is over. As soon as you rejoin Minoru, he's pushing your drink at you. "A toast," he says with a big, fake smile, "to your singing career."

"Right," you say, raising your glass and pretending to take a sip.

*Turn to page 88.*

You approach a group of middle-aged men at a nearby table. Describing Saito, you ask if anyone knows about him. The men just mumble and shake their heads. You try to ask more questions, but the dealer interrupts. "Listen, you want to play you pay. Otherwise go bother someone else."

You don't have much luck at the other tables either. You look back at the manager, who stands at the door with his arms folded. He taps his watch. Discouraged, you go home.

The next day you decide to try Sumioto's in the afternoon. You are still unable to get in, and the hostess claims never to have seen Saito.

You call the police. The detective assigned to the case tells you there are no new leads. "Don't worry," he adds, "we'll call you if anything comes up."

You go over to the dojo to ask your fellow students for help, but they can't think of what to do, and they don't seem that interested anyway.

You decide to just go to the tea shop every day and hope that Saito turns up. But you never do see him again.

**The End**

When you come to, you feel terrible. Your head is pounding, and you feel like your body weighs about three hundred pounds. You try to stand up, but the room seems to be rocking back and forth. Dizzy and weak at the knees, you lie back down.

Then you realize several sets of eyes are upon you. You find yourself on a tiny bunk in a narrow cabin. Out a circular window, you see the blue horizon line of the ocean rising and falling. You're on a boat!

As your fellow passengers come into focus, you realize they are all kids. Some are a little older than you, a few younger. A girl with blond hair comes and sits down next to you. "Are you all right?" she asks.

You nod weakly. You notice a boy over in the corner throwing up. "Poor Jeffrey," the girl says. "He's been doing that all trip."

"How long have we been out?" you ask.

"Just a couple of days. We've got a long trip in front of us."

"Where are we going?" you wonder.

The girl shrugs. "Hong Kong, probably. But they don't tell us anything."

"Why are we going to Hong Kong?"

The girl looks at you curiously. "Don't you know?" she says. "We're highly prized on the black market."

"Prized as what? Hood ornaments?"

"Domestic servants, geishas, whatever. Maybe as ornaments, too."

*Turn to page 60.*

Two days later, walking down a sidewalk in Japantown, you're startled to see Saito coming the other way. Your paths cross at a bus stop. He stops and greets you but then looks away. His face is puffy.

"What happened?" you ask bluntly.

"I've got a job. I haven't been able to come to class."

"I mean with those men who took you away."

He dismisses it with a wave of his left hand. There's something strange about him. After a moment, you realize what it is. Saito is keeping his right hand stuffed in his pocket.

A bus approaches. Saito automatically pulls his hand from his pocket for the fare. That's when you see that he's missing the top joint of his little finger. Even under the bandage, you can tell the finger is shorter than the others.

"Saito!" you gasp. "What happened to your finger?"

"Mind your own business," he snaps, stepping up to the bus. You grab the tail of his coat.

"Saito, is it a yakuza—"

You stop in midsentence, suddenly aware that people are staring at you.

"Let me go," Saito says angrily, pulling away.

Conflicting thoughts flash through your mind. You're tempted to do as Saito asks—to let him go, and just be done with him. Yet a small voice inside tells you that if you do, you'll never see him again.

---

*If you let Saito go, turn to page 91.*

*If you insist on talking to him, turn to page 79.*

"When I missed my first payment," Saito continues, "the yakuza gave me a good working over. My karate was useless against them. Besides, I'd gotten rusty. They told me I'd have to start working for them as a bouncer at the karaoke bar. And that was just to keep up with their interest payments.

"I decided to reform. I visited a famous sensei who had retired to the Marin hills, Arthur Wujan. He told me to start practicing aikido again and come back when I'd paid off my debt. I worked as a dishwasher in a coffee shop until three, I took classes at the dojo, then worked as a bouncer at Sumioto's, all in one day. But I lost patience. I decided to try a shortcut with Pai Gow again. Only this time, I wouldn't wait for luck to come. I'd cheat.

"Unfortunately, I was caught. The *oya-bun*, Hideomi, the yakuza boss, was enraged, to say the least. He said the only way I could atone was to do more of his dirty work. My first job was to go down to the waterfront with some other thugs and break up a dockworkers' strike. I did it—I beat up the union guys—but I felt terrible. That night I vowed I'd never work for the yakuza again.

"When I didn't report in to Hideomi yesterday, his men came looking for me. Up there, above Sumioto's, he said there was only one way to insure my loyalty. I had to become one of them. I would have to go through the initiation—the *yubitsume*. Then, if I ever betrayed them, they would have the right to kill me."

*Turn to page 64.*

You go back and put your ear to one of the doors. No sounds come, yet you sense something is happening inside. Then you hear it—a moan.

Suddenly, from the other side of the door, a male voice shouts, "Come on, Saito, you coward. Do it!"

Moving with smooth stealth, you try the doorknob. It turns. You crack open the door without a sound and peer in.

The scene inside is appalling. All five men in the room have their eyes riveted on Saito, who is seated at a center table. In one hand he holds a small silver knife, the little finger of the other poised underneath. He is about to undergo the yakuza initiation of yubitsume—ritual finger-cutting.

You must act quickly. You close the door and pull from your pockets the tools you may need: firecrackers, a smoke bomb, *metsubishi,* and *shuriken.* Then you tie a bandana over your mouth as a mask. Lighting the fuse on the smoke bomb, you place it in front of the door. Then you light the firecrackers and throw them down the hall. As their fuses burn down, you wedge yourself crosswise between the walls of the corridor and, alternating between your feet and hands for leverage, inch your way upward.

You're almost at ceiling height when the fuses burn to the end. Everything goes off at once. The firecrackers sound like rifles and smoke billows through the hallway.

*Turn to page 101.*

## 34

As your eyes adjust, you begin to see the man's face. It's horribly pockmarked, and a deep scar runs across his forehead. You can't imagine why he thinks anyone would want to go inside with him.

Nevertheless, he seems to be your only ticket into Sumioto's. Should you accept his invitation? you wonder. Or should you give up on trying to get in? You could go to the Pai Gow club, which was also on Saito's napkin. But you might not do any better there.

You pat your sides, reassuring yourself that your ninja tools are still there. You can take care of yourself—you think. Still, this is just the kind of trouble you feared getting into.

*If you say yes to the man, turn to page 50.*

*If you refuse his offer, turn to page 105.*

Coughing and partially blinded, you clear your eyes just in time to see four huge men bursting in from another room. They wear sleeveless T-shirts, and their rippling arm and shoulder muscles are covered with tattoos. They're yakuza!

You have no chance against the men. Three of them hold you down while the fourth runs to get Minoru. You try every trick you know, but the yakuza are just too strong.

Minoru appears a few minutes later with a needle and syringe. "Tsk, tsk," he says. "It appears our guest doesn't approve of our travel plans after all. Well, a little injection will make the journey much more pleasant."

The last thing you remember is the needle plunging into your arm.

*Turn to page 29.*

The room is filling rapidly with smoke. You pull open the sash and gulp in a couple of breaths of fresh air. Below the window, you can make out the flat roof of a garage. At least, you hope that's what it is. There's no time to be choosy. You climb through the window and leap into the dark.

You make a head-over-heels flip, landing with several rolls on the tar roof of the garage. Getting to your feet, you see Saito about to try the same thing. "No!" you cry, but he's already in the air. To your surprise, he executes the jump perfectly.

As Saito brushes himself off, you start to say, "Where did you learn—"

"Later," he cuts you off.

"Right," you agree. You find a place to climb down off the garage and escape down a dark alley. Fire sirens scream in the distance.

You keep running for several blocks until you're sure no one has followed you. Finally you stop, panting for breath. For a moment you and Saito look at one another. You're shocked when his face breaks into a smile. Holding up a pinkie, he says, "I'm grateful, right down to the tips of my fingers."

"That was a yakuza initiation ceremony, right? But why would you—"

"It's a long story," Saito breaks in. He heaves a sigh. "Don't worry, you'll get to hear it. Let's get someplace safe first—back to my apartment."

"You call that safe?" you reply. "The yakuza probably already have it staked out. No, we'd better go back to my house. Nobody's there—my family went on a camping trip."

*Turn to page 78.*

"You're right, Debbie," you say. "Let's wait for the next yakuza. This doesn't seem like it's a very big boat. There probably aren't many more of them."

You close the door and drag the unconscious man away from the door. While a couple of kids tear up sheets and tie the man up, you quietly set up a plan with Debbie and the others. Simon sits off to the side, sulking.

A few minutes later you hear a man's voice outside the door. It sounds like he's calling for his crewmate. All the kids return to their bunks. Silently you wait behind the door. The man pushes it open cautiously and steps inside. You rise behind him and give him a vicious chop to the neck.

"Two down," Debbie says, dragging him away.

"But how many to go?" you wonder.

You get two more in the same way. As Debbie starts to bind and gag the fourth man, you motion to her to wait. "He's still conscious," you say. "Let's see if we can get some information."

Once the man recovers his wits, you lean down and ask, "How many more of you are there?"

The yakuza glares at you and says something you're glad you don't understand. You grab one of his fingers and apply a ninja twist. He howls. "Just the captain and the first mate," he says when you let go.

You look up at Debbie. "I think it's time to make our move."

"Right," she says. "As soon as we get this guy tied up."

*Turn to page 71.*

Saito pauses, watching you. "I made some bad decisions, got in over my head," he explains. "I had to borrow money from the yakuza. Now it's time to pay them back. They're collecting the only way they can.

"You see," Saito goes on, "the yakuza have a problem. In Japan, guns are strictly controlled. But these days, the yakuza feel they need them to conduct business. The demand for guns in Japan is very high. The United States, meanwhile, has an abundant supply. Simple economics says hook up the demand with the supply.

"Of course," Saito continues, "they prefer not to pay for the guns. So they steal them. Then, when they have a shipment ready, they smuggle them over to Japan. But first they need someone to take the shipment down to the docks—and, if caught, to take the rap. That's where I come in. The yakuza think it's the least I can do to help work off some of my debt. That's why they picked me up the other day—to give me my assignment."

"Tell them you can't do it," you cut in. "Tell them you'll pay them back another way."

He smirks, as if at some private joke. "Just say no? If I say no, I'm a dead man."

You place your hands around your cup and think about the taste of the tea. You're stumped.

"I'm starved," Saito declares, putting both hands on the table. "Let's go get some dinner."

"Sushi?" you suggest.

"I hate sushi," he says. "Let's get a hamburger."

*Turn to page 23.*

The next morning you wake up to the sun shining through your window. But the day is quickly ruined when you remember that there are men out there who probably want to kill you.

The news gets worse when you bring in the newspaper. There is a story about the fire at Sumioto's. No one was killed, but a police detective is quoted as saying that two people are wanted for arson. Their description fits you and Saito!

Saito walks into the kitchen, yawning. You tell him the bad news. He yawns again. "It's not the police I'm worried about," he says.

"Then let's turn ourselves in," you say. "We can give them evidence about Hideomi's gang and clear ourselves of the arson charge at the same time."

Saito looks at you as if you're crazy. "As soon as we go to the police, Hideomi will know exactly where we are. Maybe we'd only spend a few nights in jail, but that'd be long enough. You think they don't have people on the inside?"

"Suppose you tell me what you propose to do then," you snap. Saito seems to be recovering from his gratitude and returning to his former self.

"I propose to die," Saito replies. You don't react, so he explains, "Not literally. But I'll stage my death for Hideomi's benefit. Then at least he won't be tracking me down. I'll have a chance to escape."

*Go on to the next page.*

You have other ideas. "Let's go to Japan, S  
If we can get to the Kurayama dojo, I know th  y  
can protect us."

"No way," Saito answers. "I told you already  
I'm not ready to go back yet."

You're exasperated. You can see he's not going  
to budge on going to Japan. But should you go  
along with his plan to stage his own death?

*If you agree to Saito's plan, turn to page 80.*

*If you try to convince him to leave the country  
instead, turn to page 72.*

At fifteen minutes before midnight, you and Saito are waiting for Hideomi on the Golden Gate Bridge. Everything is set. You're both wearing baggy pants. Underneath them is a bungy cord secured to your ankles. The other end of the cord is tied to the base of the bridge railing.

You hope Saito is right that Hideomi will never think to check for the cord. You also hope he is right that all you have to do is fall and the bungy cord will catch you. You wonder if you really want to go through with this. Luckily it's dark, and you can't see the water below.

The walkway on the bridge is lit, though, and you spot Hideomi and his men in the distance. They're wearing black suits with thin white ties and white shoes, just like in the movies. They haven't spotted you yet.

Saito makes sure the rope around your wrists appears to be bound tightly. He grabs hold of a cable and climbs up on the railing of the bridge. Then he helps you up beside him. You balance precariously on the edge of the abyss, leaning against a cable with your shoulder. It's unnerving to be without the use of your hands. The wind swirls around you.

Finally Hideomi sees you. When he's within ten feet, Saito holds up his hand, halting the approaching yakuza. He pulls a short sword from the ceremonial robe he is wearing over his clothes. It is the kind used for *seppuku*—ritual suicide.

*Turn to page 104.*

Arthur Wujan is waiting at the door for you. He's a small, bent man with long stray wisps of hair on his head and face. His pants are baggy, and his shirt hangs loose on his shoulders. His greeting is gruff, but he quickly offers you a cup of tea as he leads you to a small room next to the kitchen.

You sit cross-legged at a low table. He prepares the tea silently, and you sip it for a few minutes without saying anything. Finally Wujan asks Saito how his project is going.

"Not so well, sensei," Saito says. He looks down, then launches into the whole story of what has happened since Wujan last saw him. "We have come to seek your advice," Saito finishes humbly.

Wujan turns to you. He clears his throat. "Obviously you care about this boy whom you hardly know. Tell me honestly: is he ready to start again?"

*Turn to page 16.*

You keep still, concentrating on your balance while Hideomi's man comes up to Saito. Saito starts to hand over the sword. The man grabs his wrist and pulls him off the railing. You jump down after him.

As the yakuza inspects the sword, you hear two cars screech to a stop on the bridge. Plainclothes officers pile out, ordering everyone to freeze. Guns are suddenly in everyone's hands. Luckily, no one uses them.

Instead, as the officers approach, everyone starts screaming at once. The yakuza with the sword yells at Saito for betraying them. He plunges the sword into Saito's chest, but it simply retracts into itself. Hideomi demands the detective in charge arrest you and Saito immediately because you're the arsonists who set fire to his building. You try to tell the officer that you're guilty of nothing, and Hideomi is a yakuza.

"Shut up!" the detective shouts. "You can all do your talking down at the station." He has his men disarm and handcuff all of you. The yakuza are bundled into one car, and you and Saito into another.

Doors slam, and the detective gets in the passenger side of your car. "Let's go," he orders the driver. The driver turns on the siren and peels out.

*Turn to page 4.*

You were observing the preparation of the tea—the dark green leaves being stirred with a straw whisk in a few deft strokes—when Saito entered. You tried to keep your attention focused on the ritual, but Saito's presence made you look too hard. You weren't seeing the art in it, just the details.

"Japanese rituals are so exotic, don't you think?" Saito said.

Was this his idea of being friendly? His tone implied that you, as a *gaijin* or "foreigner," couldn't truly understand the ceremony. It was a discourteous, un-Japanese thing to say.

"I think it's a beautiful ceremony," you replied.

Saito made a snorting sound and looked on as the tea was served to you. If anything, he seemed to feel disdain for the whole thing. He seemed to have special contempt for the idea that you, an American, would appreciate it. Yet he also seemed to be trying to strike up a conversation with you. He asked how long you'd been practicing aikido. You told him.

"You have pretty good technique for a gaijin," he allowed. When you didn't reply, he went on, "Where did you study before this?"

"In Japan," you answered. "At the Kurayama family dojo."

For a moment Saito's face looked stricken. Then he recovered and continued his questions. You became uncomfortable, unsure of what he was up to. You mumbled that you had to catch the train back to Oakland and left.

*Turn to page 6.*

"I don't have to do anything I don't want to," you inform Minoru coldly, shaking your head. You have no desire to make a fool of yourself on stage.

Minoru cocks his head, smiles, and raises his glass. "To independence," he declares.

Nervously, you sip your drink. Minoru asks you questions about your family, your school, your interests. You answer without thinking, wondering how you're going to get away from him. The stituation is starting to seem very weird.

Without warning, a feeling of great excitement comes over you. You feel full of energy. You decide it would be great fun to go up on stage. You manage to say something to that effect, and Minoru lets out a big laugh. "Yes, yes," he says, standing up to pull your chair back for you. For some reason, he sounds very far away.

When you get to your feet, everything changes. You feel as if you're on a merry-go-round. The noise of the bar is suddenly very loud. The room is spinning, you are whirling, and then everything goes black.

*Turn to page 18.*

You decide to save your anger for a better target. You look over at the plate of food Minoru has left. You have to admit you're pretty hungry.

It doesn't occur to you until after you're done eating that the food might have been drugged. It's too late—that familiar feeling of sleepiness is coming over you again.

The next thing you know you're swaying back and forth, suspended in midair. You try to move your arms and legs, but you can't. You pop open one eye, but immediately close it. You glimpsed a violet dragon with big fangs, but that was enough. The dragon was a tattoo, rippling on the biceps of a burly yakuza. You're all trussed up and being carried down a flight of stairs like a sack of potatoes.

You're pretty sure they didn't see you open your eye. You pretend to be unconscious as they take you out a door. The men start to swing you back and forth as if they're going to toss you. Then you hear Minoru's voice.

"Careful with the merchandise!" he barks. The men chuckle and gently set you down on a cool metal floor. Then you hear a sliding door shut.

The engine starts, and you open your eyes. It takes a while for them to adjust, but you see that you've been stowed with a bunch of boxes in the back of a van. The van bumps over city streets and hills and finally comes to a stop. The back doors open, and you smell salt air.

"Saito!" a voice commands. "Come here and unload these boxes."

*Turn to page 12.*

You take a deep breath. "All right," you say to the man, accepting his invitation to escort you into Sumioto's.

"Excellent," he says, extending a hand. It feels scaly.

You follow him to the front door. He simply nods at the hostess, who lets you through.

"My name is Minoru," he says, once you're seated. He's wearing a cheap brown suit, you notice, with an odd pin on the lapel. "Allow me to buy you a drink."

"Soda with a lime twist," you say quickly. Even though a waitress is coming toward your table, he jumps up to get it from the bar.

While he's gone, you check out the place. It's hot, smoky, and crowded. You're the only *gaijin* there, you realize. You're used to that, but the atmosphere is different here—you don't feel welcome. Most of the patrons are young and tough-looking. The boys have their hair slicked back in severe styles. The girls wear sharp-angled jackets and vests with short skirts. Everyone is wearing a lot of leather.

You watch as two shy-looking girls go up on stage to sing a song. The DJ puts on a Japanese pop ballad. The audience groans. "Pump it up," one boys yells.

*Turn to page 20.*

You nod. You know all about the fearful yakuza from your stay in Japan, but once again you're acting impressed for Saito's sake. It's strange, you think. Something draws you to him.

But then Saito goes on, "Those men are real warriors—not like those patsies, your friends the Kurayama."

You look up sharply. "What do you know about the Kurayama family?"

"More than I want to know," Saito replies.

"And just how much is that?" you shoot back.

"Too much," he says.

You know this is a game Saito can play forever. Gesturing at the shiny black leather jacket he always wears, you say, "I guess you'd rather be with the yakuza."

"At least they believe in loyalty and honor," he retorts, getting up abruptly and leaving.

You remain seated in the tearoom, baffled. There is a double edge to Saito's words. He seems to want to befriend you, yet when you respond, he turns and attacks you. What does he want from you?

*Turn to page 9.*

As soon as you get home, you dial Nada's number again in Japan. This time the call goes through. Your heart sinks when her message machine answers. "Nada, I need to talk to you as soon as possible," you say, and slam the phone down again.

You don't have much hope the police will help. They told you they would investigate, but with so little evidence, they couldn't promise much.

You're on your own now, you realize. You unfold the piece of paper that fell out of Saito's jacket. It is a cocktail napkin. The English words at the bottom translate the Japanese characters in the center: SUMIOTO'S KARAOKE BAR.

You turn the napkin over. Handwritten on the other side is the name of a *Pai Gow* club in Oakland, the Black Dragon. Pai Gow is a Chinese game played with tiles, resembling a mixture of poker and blackjack. There is also a strange, hand-drawn symbol underneath: inscribed in a diamond are two swords alongside some Japanese characters you can't make out.

You turn the napkin over again, thinking back on Saito's words about the yakuza. The men who took him away sure looked like gangsters. The evidence of the *karaoke* bar and gambling club back this up.

*Turn to page 13.*

You take four guns out of the box. When Saito appears behind the controls of the forklift, you motion him into the van. He has to come in anyway to load the boxes onto the fork. You hand him two of the guns.

Saito looks at you in disbelief. "Are you insane?"

You give him a hard stare. "Whose side are you on anyway?"

"Mine," he mutters, but he takes the guns. You help him load the boxes onto the fork, leaving a space for yourself behind them. You climb onto the forklift and motion Saito to back out.

Saito backs away from the van. He raises the fork with you hidden behind the boxes. You climb up to peer over the boxes. Unfortunately, at that very moment one of the yakuza is looking you straight in the eyes.

"Freeze!" you say, climbing up on top of the boxes, a gun in each hand. Only you know that they're empty.

You survey the dock. All motion has stopped. There are a lot more yakuza here than you expected. Each one of them has a hand poised inside his jacket.

Saito jumps off the forklift. His guns are aimed at an older man. "Tell them to throw out their weapons, Hideomi," Saito says to him.

Hideomi looks at him defiantly. "Go ahead and kill me, Saito. You know I'd rather die than surrender to a punk like you."

*Go on to the next page.*

Then everything seems to happen at once. Several of Hideomi's men pull their guns and start to fire at you. The bullets thunk into the boxes in front of you. You turn the guns in your hand around and, grasping them between your thumb and forefinger, sling them like *shuriken* at two of the yakuza, knocking the guns from their hands.

Out of the corner of your eye, to your amazement, you see Saito do the same thing. The firing stops temporarily. You climb on top of the boxes, gauge the distance to the edge of the dock, and leap into the cold water of the bay.

*Turn to page 5.*

You can't just abandon Saito to his abductors, you decide. Even though you have misgivings, you head down to the BART station to catch the train into the city. Before you leave, you pack a few ninja tools into the hidden inner pockets of your clothing, just in case.

In downtown San Francisco, you decide not to waste time on a bus. You hail a cab and give the address for Sumioto's Karaoke Bar. The driver looks at you and says, "Are you sure?" You hand him five dollars and tell him to get going.

As he pulls up in front of the bar, you pay the remainder of the fare. The driver just shakes his head as he takes your money. You are in an exceedingly dismal part of town. The sign for Sumioto's blinks on and off, and you head straight for it.

The hostess at the door wears an elegant silk kimono. She is young, her lips made up in red. They set in a hard line as soon as she sees you. "Identification, please," she says.

You start to explain that you're looking for a friend and just need to ask him a few questions. Her eyes glaze over in incomprehension. You switch to Japanese, but she doesn't want to hear it. "I'll need to see some ID," she repeats, brushing you aside to greet the next set of patrons.

*Turn to page 15.*

"Nice of you to finally talk to me," you say.

"I was going to call you tomorrow," she protests sleepily.

"Listen," you say, and proceed to explain very quickly what has happened. You can tell, across five thousand miles of ocean, she's flabbergasted. She wants to hear more, but you cut her off. "I'll tell you more when it doesn't cost ten dollars a minute. Just tell me how to get there—assuming I can convince Saito to come."

"I'll call you back within the hour," Nada promises.

*Turn to page 100.*

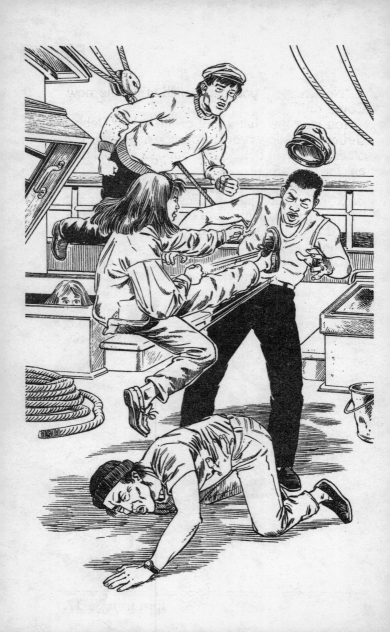

"No waiting!" you declare. "Let's strike now. Come on!"

You lead the charge out of the cabin. Debbie shrugs and follows you, inspecting the pistol. The other kids fall in behind her, but you can tell they are full of doubt.

A narrow stairway appears to lead up to the deck. "I'll go and stir up some trouble," you say. "The rest of you come up in sixty seconds. Debbie, you don't have to actually use that thing—just pretend you will."

You bound up the steps and break out onto the deck, ready for anything. A grizzled deckhand looks at you curiously. You fell him with a single blow to the solar plexus. Two more come running at you. You jump high in the air, flooring each of them with a kick. Then a voice behind you barks, "Stop! Stop right there!"

*Turn to page 17.*

"Wait a minute," you say, your head beginning to clear. "What you're saying is that we're going to be slaves!"

"Brilliant, Sherlock," a red-haired boy says.

"And the yakuza are the slave traders," you say. "It's all starting to make sense. Minoru is their recruiter."

"They have lots of recruiters," the boy says. "You must have given them some trouble. You've been out cold for two days."

"I'll give them a lot more trouble soon," you say.

"Wait a minute," the boy says. "That's the last thing we need. Out here in the middle of the ocean—who's going to help us? These guys have guns, not to mention knives, poisons, and who knows what else. Just take it easy, at least until we get into port."

"I'm not taking it easy," you reply. "Right now we have the advantage of numbers. Once we're in port, they'll split us up. We'll have no money and no transportation. We're still within two days of San Francisco."

"You *are* a troublemaker," the boy says. "No wonder they doped you up."

"But Simon, it's true," the blond girl says. "Are we just going to let this happen to us?"

"Give me a break, Debbie," he replies. "What chance do we have against these guys?"

"We'll find out soon enough," you say. Someone is unlocking the hatch to the cabin. All eyes are on you as you race to the door.

*Turn to page 94.*

You move back down from the edge of the roof and press yourself into the shadows against the wall. Japanese voices whisper urgently to one another. You stay completely still as they look over the spot you just occupied. Then they move away.

Cautiously you pull yourself back up over the lip. In the rooftop moonlight, you can see two men. Their hair is short, and they are wearing sleeveless T-shirts, yet their shoulders seem swathed in color. With a start you realize they are tattooed. The men must be yakuza!

What are they doing here? Are they backups for the job? Or do they have some other purpose— like trying to hijack the gun shipment?

You are startled to hear Kurt hiss at you from below, "Can we come up yet?" You almost shush him, but you hold your breath. The footsteps of the two men quickly approach the roof edge. Your friends have been discovered.

What now? You can try to escape, or you can take on the two yakuza yourself. Your decision depends partly on why you think they are there. If they're Hideomi's men, you don't want to have anything to do with them. But if they're not, you may be able to convince them to team up with you.

One of the men shines a flashlight toward Kurt and Keiku. They still don't know you're there. You have about three seconds to decide what to do.

*If you decide to confront the men, turn to page 106.*

*If you decide to keep silent, turn to page 98.*

## 62

You're going to kick down these walls, but not just yet. You'll wait and listen to make sure Minoru has left first.

You wait nearly an hour. It doesn't sound like anything is happening outside. Carefully you choose a spot in the wall between two studs. Then you back up.

With three steps you deliver a flying double-heel kick to the wall, smashing in a hole the size of a basketball. It's incredibly satisfying. You proceed with a blinding series of kicks and punches, destroying a space in the wall large enough for your body to fit through. Plaster dust is flying all over the place, making you cough.

You still have to get through the plaster on the other side of the studs, but you don't waste time with more kicks. You simply attack it with three powerful head-butts. The wall crumbles. On the third one you break through, falling forward into the next room.

*Turn to page 35*.

"Luckily," Saito finishes, "you came along just in time. I was seconds away from becoming a yakuza."

"The bad news is, they probably still want to kill you—and now me as well," you comment. "Not only did we burn down the bar, we don't know if Hideomi survived."

Saito shrugs. "Right now all I care about is that I have a reprieve. I just wish I knew what to do next."

"So do I," you say. You pause, giving Saito a penetrating look. He refuses to meet your eyes. "You're not telling me everything. Tonight, when we jumped from the window—where did you learn the art of the ninja?"

Saito hangs his head. "I might as well tell you," he murmurs. "You see, I was not so surprised to discover that you knew ninjutsu. After all, anyone who studied with the Kurayama . . ."

His voice trails off. You have to lean forward to hear what he says next. "You see, I too am a Kurayama. Your friend Nada—is my first cousin."

You let out a long, slow breath. It all begins to make sense. Except for one thing. "I don't understand," you say. "When you got into trouble, why didn't you go back? They're a forgiving family. I know they'd take you—"

Saito holds up his hand to stop you. "Yes. They might take me back. But it is my choice. It is my pride. I will go back when I am ready."

You want to argue, but you are tired. "Let's sleep on it," you say. "We can decide what to do in the morning.

*Turn to page 40.*

Saito reluctantly agrees that the plan just might work. You don't mention to him that you're also going to try to bring some help.

You go home and call your friends Kurt and Keiku from the dojo. They agree to help you out. Then, before you go to bed, you open a bag you have not unpacked since your return from Japan. It contains all the ninja tools you'll need for tomorrow night.

You meet Kurt and Keiku at the dojo the next afternoon. Kurt has a car, and you arrange to have them pick you up in three hours. After class, you walk a few blocks down to the police station. You have an appointment with Detective Liu, the officer who was investigating Saito's disappearance.

After setting things up with Detective Liu, you walk a few blocks more to Saito's apartment. He buzzes you in the front door, and you climb a dark stairway to the third floor. The apartment is small, little more than a room with a bed and a utility kitchen.

*Turn to page 84.*

"We can't jump!" you cry to Saito. "Let's take the stairs."

Without giving him a chance to answer, you pull Saito out of the door. But, blinded by the smoke, he stumbles over the inert bodies in the hallway. You help him up, but now the smoke from the fire is starting to overcome you.

No sooner do you get going again than you run smack into the first two men who came out the door. You can't believe they've come back up the stairs—until the word *giri* flashes through your mind: loyalty. The men must have come back for their boss and comrades. It doesn't occur to you that perhaps they've come back for revenge.

You try to slip by them, thinking they want only to get back to the room. But one of them pistol-whips you on the back of the head, and the other knocks out Saito.

You're only half-conscious as they drag you down the hall and throw you into a closet. Vaguely, somewhere in the back of your mind, you hear the door being locked. In this room, there are no windows. But you're lucky in one respect—by the time the flames reach you, you're totally unconscious.

**The End**

"Saito and Hideomi will arrive any minute," you say to Keiku and Kurt. "Climb up the fire escape and back us up if we have any trouble."

Your two friends nod, and you race off to the other side of the building. The van comes squealing around the corner just as you hide in a doorway. Hideomi gets out of the passenger door, all business. Saito gets out more slowly.

Hideomi strides to the dock edge and peers across the water. "Look for the trawler," he instructs Saito. "It should be here soon."

"I doubt there is any trawler," you say, emerging from the darkened doorway. You hold a ten-foot *kusari-fundo,* or ninja chain, across the palms of your hands.

Hideomi just turns and smiles, as if he's been expecting you. He whistles up to the warehouse roof.

"Your men aren't there any more," you inform him. Kurt and Keiku appear at the edge.

Without a word, Hideomi reaches inside his coat. You swing the chain twice over your head. Before Hideomi can pull his gun, you throw the chain. It wraps his arms tightly to his sides.

*Go on to the next page.*

Saito looks at you in shock. The first words out of his mouth are "You're a ninja!" Then he looks from the water to the warehouse roof to Hideomi. "This whole thing was a setup?"

"A test of your loyalty," you say. "We found two of Hideomi's men on the roof. There are probably more on the way, but we can let Detective Liu deal with them."

"So that's why you came along," Saito says to Hideomi. "To tempt me into betraying you."

"And you did!" Hideomi spits at Saito. "But don't worry—you'll never escape us."

*Turn to page 97.*

You bring Debbie and her pistol with you, leaving the others to guard your prisoners.

"Are you willing to act as bait?" you ask as you steal up the narrow stairway outside the door.

"As long as you keep doing the dirty work," she says cheerfully.

"Give me about a minute," you say. "Then go up to the pilothouse and call the captain and first mate. Stand just outside the door—be sure not to go in. I just hope they're both together."

Silently you creep up the stairs and poke your head out on deck. All seems quiet. Keeping low, you scamper the length of the boat. In a flash you climb to the top of the wheelhouse, making hardly a sound.

Debbie appears down on the deck. Holding the pistol in front of her, she cautiously approaches the house, then calls in, "Hey you sleazeballs! Get out here. I'm hijacking this boat!"

A man's head appears just below you. "What's this, a mutiny?" he chuckles.

"That's right," Debbie says. She cocks the gun.

The captain calls over his shoulder, "Hey, George, come on out here. Our cargo is getting uppity!"

Another man's head appears below you. "Now, let's see how serious you are about this mutiny," the captain says to Debbie.

"You don't really want to pull that trigger, do you?" the mate adds.

The two men advance on her. She backs up, looking worried.

*Turn to page 96.*

"There's no way I'm helping you die, staged or not," you tell Saito. "It's too dangerous. We've got to get out of the country."

"I'm not going back to Japan," he responds angrily.

"Fine," you say, trying to keep him calm. "I'll get a flight to Vancouver." It's the closest foreign city you can think of.

"As long as it doesn't cost more than $17.50," he shoots back, "because that's all I've got. Maybe we can catch on with a flock of Canadian geese."

Saito stalks out of the room. You're flustered. How are you going to pay for an airplane flight?

In spite of your promise, you decide to call Nada. Your call goes through, and luckily she is there. It's the middle of the night; she answers after several rings.

*Turn to page 57.*

You follow Saito to Liu's car while Liu gets the rest of the yakuza packed off.

"This may come as a shock to you," Saito warns. "But I'm a ninja, too. In fact—I'm a Kurayama."

You try to act surprised, but you know Saito sees through it. You admit to seeing the Kurayama family seal while you were waiting in his apartment. "Once I knew you were a Kurayama, I figured you also had to be a ninja."

Saito asks how you know the family. You tell him about Nada and the time you spent at the family dojo. Saito's eyes seem to light up as you talk. "Nada is my best friend in the world," you finish.

"And she's my first cousin!" Saito exclaims. Then he looks sad. "She was one of the ones I couldn't face after I dishonored the family. I worked as a ninja-for-hire—a mercenary. I didn't realize how badly the family would look upon it."

Saito pauses, looking out over the bay. "I think I'm ready to go back," he says after a while. "I'll make a clean breast of it, tell the family everything that's happened. They can decide for themselves whether to take me back."

"I'll back you up," you promise. "In fact, this might be just the excuse I need to go back to Japan!"

**The End**

You find Saito upstairs reading your brother's comic books. "Get ready," you say to him. "We're leaving in five minutes."

"Where to?" he asks.

"Anywhere but here," you reply.

You go back downstairs and call a taxi. Ten minutes later a honk comes from outside. "Let's go," you call up to Saito.

You jump in the cab and tell the driver, "Port of Oakland. Berth 83."

Saito looks at you in alarm. "I'm not getting on any boats," he exclaims. "I'll get seasick!"

"Don't worry," you say, pretending to lower your voice for secrecy. "It's only to Vancouver."

The taxi drops you at the security gate to the port. "Pay the man," you order Saito, figuring that the less money he has, the less likely he'll be to take off.

While Saito reluctantly pays, you tell the guard you're here to see Captain Tanaka of the *Okuri*. "You'd better hurry," he says. "The tugboats are coming to undock them right now."

You grab Saito's hand and run through a maze of new cars that has just been taken off another ship. Up ahead, the *Okuri* looms. It's a gigantic container ship, with a tall, straight black hull. A huge crane is loading freight containers onto the deck. The containers look like play blocks.

*Turn to page 103.*

You ask for the manager, and moments later a stocky man in suspenders comes out puffing on a cigar. You ask him about Saito. His face darkens. "You a friend of his?" he asks.

"Sort of," you say.

"Then you're not welcome here," he snaps, turning you by the shoulders to leave.

"Wait, wait," you say. "Saito may be in trouble—with the yakuza."

"Wouldn't surprise me a bit," the manager says unhelpfully.

"Can I just check with some of the players to find out if they know anything?"

The manager looks at his watch. "I'll give you five minutes. And I'll have my eye on you every minute."

"Thanks a lot," you murmur.

*Turn to page 28.*

But that night when you get home, you find you're unable to sleep. You toss and turn in bed, trying to think of a way to get Saito out of his predicament. He's being too hard on himself, you think. He seems determined to punish himself for his mistakes.

There's one last straw you can grasp. Arthur Wujan is a legendary sensei. You doubt he'd take the time to help you, but he did tell Saito he might take him on as a student. If you can get Saito to visit him again, maybe he can help find a way out.

You wake up at six. Luckily Saito's number is in the directory. He answers the phone almost immediately. "Are you awake?" you ask.

"Yes," he admits. "I didn't sleep too well."

Sensing that Saito's mood has changed, you waste no time. You propose your idea of going to see Arthur Wujan for advice right away. Saito agrees it's a good idea. "I'll pick you up at the BART station on my scooter," he says.

You quickly dress. An hour later, you're on the back of Saito's scooter crossing the Golden Gate Bridge. Fog swirls through the towers. Every once in a while you get a glimpse of the waves crashing below.

Once you're in Marin County, Saito takes a narrow, winding road that climbs higher and higher into the hills. He turns off on a tiny dirt road and bumps down to a modest wood house set in a clump of live oaks. Saito points to an addition on the house that's as large as the original. "That's the dojo," he says.

*Turn to page 44.*

You get to the BART station just in time to catch the last train to Oakland. Once home, with the doors and windows locked, you finally relax. You make a pot of tea for Saito and yourself. Without any prompting, he starts telling you his story.

Born into a respected family with a long *bujutsu* tradition, from an early age Saito excelled at the martial arts. Before long he was groomed to take over the family dojo.

"But two years ago I made a mistake," he says. "I hired out my services. I figured, why live like a monk? I just wanted a few of the good things in life. My family didn't appreciate it at all. They said I was a mere mercenary, I had disgraced their name.

"I was fed up with tradition. I left Japan to make a new start in this country. It was easy to find work teaching karate, but it wasn't enough. I got bored. I guess I lost my way. I started hanging out with what you might call the wrong sort of people—staying out late, shooting pool, and that kind of stuff. My downfall, though, was getting hooked on Pai Gow—a Chinese game kind of like poker or blackjack."

"At the Black Dragon," you put in.

Saito looks at you, surprised, then goes on, "Right. At first I did very well. I could sense what was going to happen. But the late nights took a toll on me and I lost my touch. I began to lose. But the more I lost, the more I played, trying to win it back. Needless to say I lost even more. I owed way more than I could pay. So I borrowed from the only place I could—the yakuza."

*Turn to page 31.*

You tug hard on Saito's coat, pulling him off the first step of the bus. He turns as if to hit you, but you look him directly in the eyes. He lowers his arm.

"Let's have a cup of tea," you say, leading him away from the bus. He brushes your hand away but walks along with you. He looks both annoyed and relieved.

You find a table and order. Saito heaves a big sigh, then stares off out the window. You're not sure what to say. "So what's your new job?" you venture.

It takes him a while to answer. "Oh, it's just . . ." he trails off, still staring out the window.

Suddenly he looks directly at you. "Stealing guns," he blurts.

"Where, um, where do you steal them from?"

Saito bursts into laughter. "The art of polite conversation," he comments. "The question is not where, but why."

"I was getting to that," you say. Saito looks down into his tea. You can't help staring at his bandaged finger. "Who were those men who took you away?" you ask quietly.

"You've already figured it out—they're yakuza," he admits.

"But why did they attack you like that?"

He sips his tea. "Because I owe them money."

*Turn to page 39.*

"How are you going to trick Hideomi into believing you're dead?" you ask.

Saito outlines his plan to you. You stare at him and say quietly, "You're insane."

"I know," he replies. "But it's the only thing that's going to save my life."

"Do you really expect me to trust this 'bungy cord' thing to catch me?"

"Believe me, they work. People jump from great heights with them all the time."

Without waiting for your accord, he picks up the telephone. You can understand most of what he's saying in Japanese. Fear fills his face, and you know he's talking to Hideomi. "A thousand apologies oya-bun," he says. "I am grieved by the injury to your arm. I will prove that this was not my desire. I will prove my eternal loyalty to you. I will sacrifice my own arm—no, my whole life to you."

Saito listens as Hideomi speaks. Looking at you, he says he has you in captivity. Yes, he says, he will bring you. Suddenly you feel nervous.

"Yes, oya-bun, the Golden Gate Bridge. At midnight," Saito says, then hangs up.

Saito looks at you triumphantly. "It's going to work," he tells you. "Of course he said he didn't believe me. But I could hear in his voice that he felt differently. He is so egotistical, he wants to believe I would actually kill myself for him."

Saito sets off to find a pair of bungy cords and the other props he will need to stage his event, while you make a couple of calls of your own. It never hurts to have a backup plan, you think.

*Turn to page 42.*

You're not going to stick your neck out for Saito. The situation is too dangerous, and you have too few clues. As you get ready for bed, you try to just forget about him.

You wake up in the morning and go about your business, but the image of Saito being punched yesterday keeps coming back. You know how well trained he is in self-defense. Anyone who could do that to him can't be good.

Soon it's time to take the train into San Francisco. On your way to the dojo, you stop by the police station to drop off the cocktail napkin. No one there seems very interested in the piece of evidence you have. They tell you that most of the time a missing person case solves itself. You reply that Saito's not missing, he's kidnapped.

At the dojo, you tell your fellow students what happened yesterday. They're surprised; no one has any idea what it could be about, but they don't seem very interested in trying to find out. No one knows, or likes, Saito very well. They advise you not to worry, it will sort itself out.

You try to put the whole thing out of your mind. But you don't feel good about it.

*Turn to page 30.*

Your gaze wanders back to the stage, to a slickly dressed pair of boys singing a Michael Jackson song. They swivel their hips and do a pretty decent moonwalk. Looking back at the bar, you see no sign of Minoru or your waitress. You wonder what's going on.

Someone prods you in the ribs. You look behind to see a boy smiling at you and gesturing at the now empty stage. "Your turn," he says.

You freeze, about to shake your head definitely no. Then you feel another prod, and Minoru is suddenly beside you. You wonder if you should have taken your chance to slip away when you had it.

Minoru points to the stage. "Go ahead," he says with a big smile. "Show us your talents."

"I don't want to sing," you say tersely.

Minoru tuts reprovingly. "But you must. What's the American saying—you must sing for your dinner?"

Everyone looks at you expectantly. You don't like feeling pressured, but something in you also says, why not?

If you decide to go up on stage,
turn to page 26.

If you shake your head no, turn to page 47.

Exhausted, you sit shivering under a eucalyptus tree. Now you have a chance to ask Saito the question that's been on your mind for over an hour. "So you're a ninja," you say point-blank.

Saito can't suppress his smile. "You too," he says. "But I'm not surprised. Once I heard you studied with the Kurayama family, I expected as much."

"And you?" you ask.

You have to lean very close to hear Saito murmur, "I, too, am a Kurayama."

You look at him in shock. He proceeds to tell you a long story about how he came to be here. It seems that at one time he was part of the respected Kurayama family of Japan, first cousin to your friend Nada. But he disgraced himself by selling his services as a ninja and decided to leave Japan for San Francisco. Falling on hard times, he got involved in gambling and had to borrow money from the yakuza. When he couldn't pay it back, they forced him to join their ranks. That's how he came to help them smuggle guns—among other things—out of the city.

"Perhaps it's time to go back to your family," you say quietly.

"Yes," he says, "I think maybe it is."

**The End**

As Saito brews you a cup of tea on a hot plate, you notice he looks worried. When you ask him why, he explains, "It's been a long time since I've done anything like this. Anything that might require fighting, that is. I'm not sure I'm up to it."

It's unlike Saito to express such doubts. Suddenly you realize that must have been why he was so aggressive in class—to make up for his insecurities. "Don't worry," you tell him. "I just talked to Detective Liu. He'll be there. We won't have to do any fighting."

You go over the plan one more time with Saito. You're not really sure that there will be no fighting, but your words help him relax. Saito glances at his watch. "It's time for me to go. Wish me luck—wish *us* luck."

You have an hour to kill before Kurt and Keiku show up. Idly you let your gaze wander up and down Saito's desk. Something in a half-opened drawer catches your eye. You pull out a yellowed piece of parchment. At the top of the page is the crest of the Kurayama family.

You glance over the parchment, your heart pounding. Although you can speak Japanese fairly well, your reading knowledge is limited. But you can make out enough to realize one thing: Saito is a Kurayama. Suddenly it seems as if a lot more is at stake tonight than catching some yakuza.

*Turn to page 93.*

Finally Saito was forced to borrow money from the only place he could get it—the yakuza. When he failed to make his first loan payment, the *oya-bun*, or yakuza boss, put him to work as a bouncer at Sumioto's Karaoke Bar.

Saito knew that he'd be in trouble if he got too involved with the yakuza. So he vowed to reform. He visited a reclusive sensei named Arthur Wujan in the hills of Marin and told him he wanted to become his disciple. Wujan told him to return when he had worked off his debt.

Saito went to work eighteen hours a day: he washed dishes in a restaurant, began practicing aikido, and worked at the bar at night. But he decided he needed a shortcut. He went back to the Pai Gow club. This time he was sure he could win—he would cheat.

The only hitch was he got caught. Hideomi, the yakuza oya-bun, was furious. He forced Saito to take on rougher jobs for the gang. He was sent down to the waterfront with some other thugs to break up a dockworkers' strike. They succeeded, but after that night Saito vowed never to work for the yakuza again.

"They changed my mind pretty fast, though," Saito says. "You saw their method of inviting me over for a chat. Hideomi decided it was time for me to become one of them. He forced me to go through the initiation, which included cutting off the tip of my finger in order to prove my loyalty. He also gave me my first job, which is this gun-smuggling run. It's set for tomorrow night."

*Go on to the next page.*

"But can't you pay them back? Why don't you sell your scooter? Or—I'll help you," you volunteer.

Saito laughs. "My scooter wouldn't even cover the first payment. Besides, it's too late," he says, holding up his finger. "I can't go back. Once you've been initiated, you're bound for life. It's called *giri*—obligation."

"But you didn't really mean it when you got initiated, did you?"

Saito shrugs. "That doesn't matter. In their eyes, if I betray them, they have the right to kill me."

*Turn to page 24.*

"Listen," you say to Minoru, "can you take me upstairs? I want to see the manager."

Minoru raises his eyebrows. "Sure," he says, after thinking about it. "Finish your drink, and I'll take you up."

"No," you say firmly, "I want to go now."

Minoru gives you a strange look, then he shrugs. "Okay, we'll go now."

You follow him as he winds his way through the bar, making it a point to greet everyone he passes, trying to impress you. Your waitress gives you a worried look as you go by.

You nearly bump into Minoru as he stops to fumble with a door at the back of the bar. This gives you a chance to get a closer look at the pin on his lapel. You recognize it—it's the same design drawn on Saito's cocktail napkin. Now you know you're on the scent.

Minoru gets the door open and leads you up a flight of creaky wooden stairs. As you reach the top, you tap him on the back as if to ask a question. The moment he turns, you deliver a swift punch to his solar plexus. A brief look of shock crosses his face, then he crumples in a corner.

Now you're in ninja mode. You move silently down the narrow hallway, stopping to listen at each door. You hear nothing. Another flight of stairs lies at the end of the hall, but you hesitate.

*Turn to page 33.*

"Let's not waste any time—let's try to trap the yakuza tomorrow night," you say to Saito. "I'll help you."

"No way," Saito responds. "You're not getting mixed up in this."

"Listen, Saito, you can't do it alone. You at least need a backup. Besides, I've got a plan."

Saito regards you skeptically. "What's your plan?"

You think furiously. "Will Hideomi be with you?"

"Yes," Saito says, "which is kind of unusual. But I guess he wants to watch my work firsthand."

"So what's the deal? Where do you pick up the shipment?"

"The guns are waiting in a garage on Geary Street. I'm supposed to meet Hideomi at his headquarters. We'll go to the garage, load up the guns, and take them down to the docks. A trawler waiting offshore will signal when they're ready to take on cargo."

"Okay, here's what we'll do," you say, and proceed to outline your plan.

*Turn to page 65.*

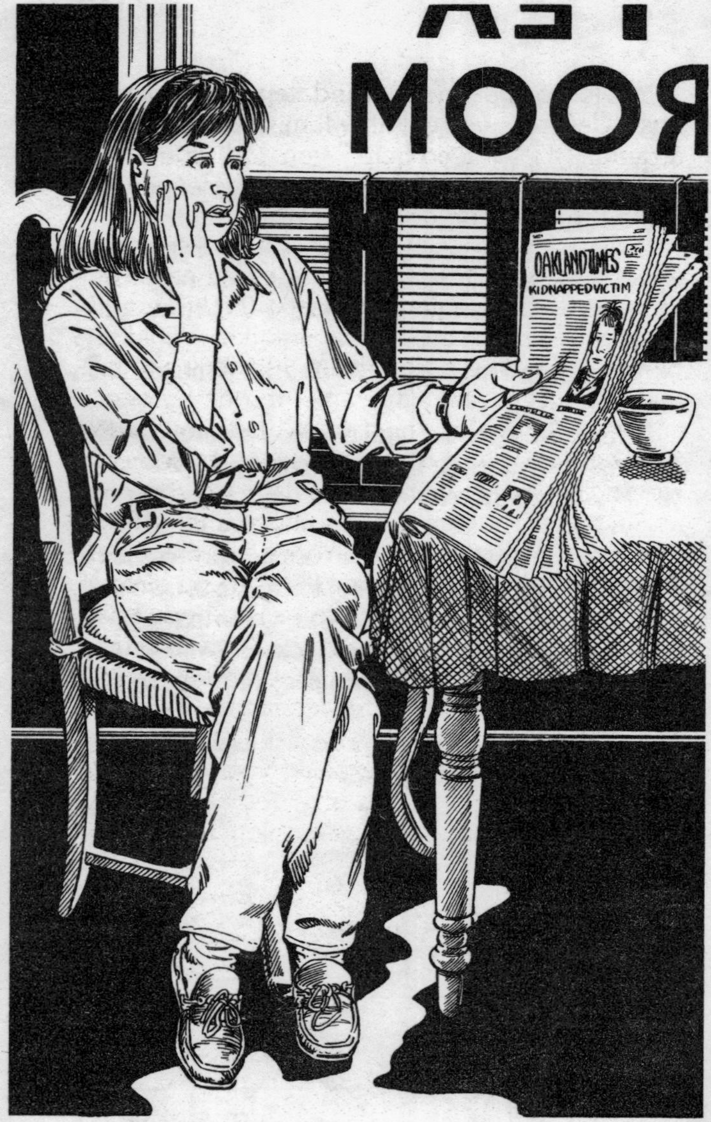
OAKLAND TIMES
KIDNAPPED VICTIM

You let go of Saito's coat and step away from the bus. "Call me," you say after him. He doesn't turn around. "If you need help," you add. You're not sure if he heard you. The rest of the passengers file on to the bus. The doors whoosh shut.

Walking over to the tearoom, you feel strangely depressed. You order tea and a sweet cake, but they don't taste right. You leave the cake half-eaten and wander around Japantown. A cold fog blows in from the ocean. Darkness begins to fall, and the lights in the city come on one by one.

Every day for the next week you stop at the tearoom after class. You stay as long as you can, reading the newspaper, hoping Saito will show up.

But there is no sign of him—that is until you see his picture in the newspaper. Your heart sinks like a stone. As you read the story, it's as if you already know what it will say. Police found his body floating in the bay. They believe his death is tied to crime syndicate activity, and that he may be the same man who was reported kidnapped in Japantown ten days earlier.

For reasons you can't explain, you feel terribly bad about the death of this man you barely knew. You'll never escape the feeling you could have helped him.

**The End**

The steward brings you three meals a day. It's quite comfortable, except for Saito's cold silence.

You're stuck inside with him all day, but at night, when things are quiet, you come out on deck. The stars overhead are brilliant, and the black water churns under the ship. The seagoing life isn't so bad, you decide.

Apparently Saito has been having similar thoughts. One night he suddenly breaks the silence. "I'm not getting off the ship," he says. "The second mate told me I could sign on. We're going to Stockholm next."

You say nothing. Saito goes on, "A couple of years at sea will be good for me. It'll earn me enough money to pay off my debts. It'll give the yakuza a chance to forget about me. And I'll get to see the world."

"Sounds great," you say. "Except for one thing—your family. There'll be a few days' layover in Yokohama. Come with me to the dojo. You don't have to stay for more than a day. I know Nada can't wait to see you."

Saito looks at you as if you're crazy. His lips twitch a little, and you realize he's trying to keep from smiling. Reluctantly he agrees.

You lean against the railing and look out over the ocean. Everything suddenly seems to be working out. Saito will have a chance to make a new start and reconcile with his family. As for you, you've gotten a free trip to Japan out of the deal.

**The End**

Before you know it, the door buzzer sounds. You grab your bag, lock the door behind you, and run down the stairs. Kurt has the car running. "Do you have your camera?" you ask Keiku. She nods.

Kurt drives carefully over the hills of San Francisco. You've got plenty of time. You cross Market Street and roll down the wide avenues of the warehouse district. After you cross the railroad tracks, the dark waters of the bay are in front of you.

You tell Kurt where to park. Hoisting your bag over your shoulder, you lead your two friends through darkened alleys toward the waterfront. The pungent smell of the bay grows stronger.

Soon you hear the sound of lapping water. You go along the dockside until you find the warehouse number you want. An iron fire escape climbs its back. You pull a *kaginawa* from your bag, swing it in a loop, and toss it up toward the fire ladder. It hooks on the bottom rung, and you climb the rope. Gesturing to Kurt and Keiku to wait, you silently ascend the iron stairway to the roof of the warehouse.

As you begin to pull yourself over the lip, your sharp eyes pick up some movement. You drop back down just enough to peer over the edge. Two bulky figures are on the roof, you notice—and they're coming in your direction.

*Turn to page 61.*

As soon as the door opens and you see a hand, you grab it. You twist it over your back and flip the owner over the top. He lands with a big thud and doesn't move.

Everyone stares at the unconscious man. Simon's eyes are wide with fear. You pat the man's pockets and remove a pistol. Tossing it to Debbie, you say, "Are you with me?"

Her eyes widen as the gun sails toward her. She catches it and turns it over cautiously in her hands. "Yes," she says, "but—"

"But what?" you demand. "Let's go. All of us. There's no way they can stop us."

"I think we should wait," Debbie says hesitantly. "Let's wait until another comes down. That way we can get them one by one."

"We should attack while we have the momentum," you reply. What you don't say is that you don't want to give Debbie and the other kids time to have second thoughts.

Then again, Debbie might have a point. By waiting you may be able to eliminate two or three more yakuza before you take on the whole boat.

*If you decide to wait for the next yakuza, turn to page 38.*

*If you want to lead the attack now, turn to page 59.*

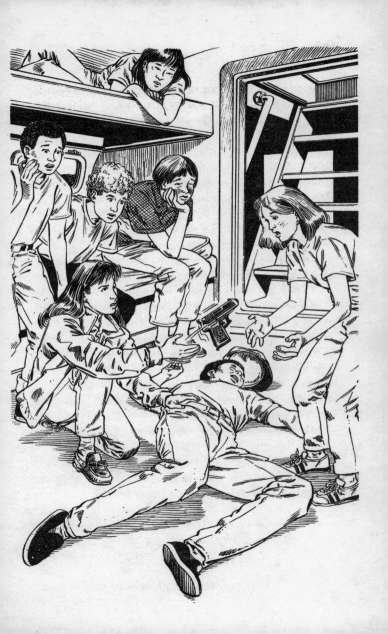

With a bone-chilling yell, you leap from the top of the wheelhouse. You catch both men on the shoulders, knocking them to the ground. The captain gets up, aiming a fist at your face, but your lightning-fast jab to his kidneys doubles him over, and a blow to his neck knocks him out.

"Hold it!" the mate says. You whirl to see him aiming a pistol at your heart. "We should have gotten rid of you a long time ago," he snarls.

Suddenly his head snaps, and he falls forward to the deck. Debbie stands behind him, holding the butt of the pistol which has just been applied to the mate's neck. She looks at the gun curiously.

"Thanks," you say.

Suddenly the rest of the kids are on deck, clapping and cheering and skipping around, even Simon. They drag the captain and first mate downstairs and make sure the whole lot of them are locked up. Debbie takes the helm. Someone else starts playing with the radio, sending out a Mayday. Eventually the Coast Guard responds, saying help is on the way.

The seas are quiet, and all of you sit back to enjoy the trip. You're still not sure what happened to Saito, but you've bagged yourself a band of yakuza. You can only hope that when the police investigate, they'll turn up your friend.

**The End**

Detective Liu's car comes screeching onto the dock. He and two officers jump out, their pistols drawn. When they see you, they lower their guns.

"Doesn't look like you need our help," Liu comments as he slaps handcuffs on Hideomi. "Our squad cars intercepted the rest of the gang a few blocks away. They're in the paddy wagon already."

Liu motions to the two officers to take Hideomi away. Again Hideomi repeats his threat to Saito. "Don't worry," Liu assures Saito. "We'll put you in a witness protection program."

Keiku and Kurt come down from the warehouse roof. They tell Liu about the other two yakuza in the back alley. "Any sign of the trawler?" he asks them.

They shake their heads. "I doubt there ever was one," you say. "The whole operation was to test Saito."

"And I passed with flying colors," Saito remarks sarcastically.

Liu lets his hands flop to his sides. "I guess that's it then. Saito, you can come with us. As for the rest of you, we'll be in touch."

"Wait," Saito says, grabbing your arm. "Come with us. There's something I want to tell you."

*Turn to page 73.*

You keep perfectly still as the two yakuza peer down from the roof. They still haven't seen you. One of them clambers onto the fire escape. You grab his leg, twist it, and flip him onto the metal landing below. He's out cold.

You swing over to the other side and pull yourself up to the roof just as something hard and metal clangs against the spot on the wall you just left. The moment you land on the roof, you crouch and roll to your left. The other yakuza turns and swings at you with the metal club, just missing you. You spring to your feet. He comes at you again, but you keep twisting and dodging backward, avoiding his strikes.

Something tells you you're nearing the edge of the warehouse. Instinctively, you know your next move. As the yakuza lunges at you again, you pitch yourself forward, cutting him down at his feet. Surprised, he can't stop his momentum. He goes flying over you and the edge of the building. A second later you hear a big splash.

Running back to the fire escape, you hear Kurt's voice. "What's going on?" he cries.

"A couple of Hideomi's men were waiting for us up here," you explain breathlessly. "I'll take care of the one on the fire escape. You two go fish the other one out of the water and tie him up."

You have plenty of rope in your bag. The man on the fire escape is still unconscious. You bind him securely to the grillwork. By the time you're done, Keiku and Kurt have brought over the other man, bound and gagged and dripping wet.

*Turn to page 68.*

Forty-five minutes later the phone rings. "Here's the plan," Nada says. "A close friend of the family is in the shipping business. One of their vessels, the *Okuri*, is in port in Oakland right now. The thing is, it's about to leave. Its destination is the port of Yokohama, in Japan. I'll be there to meet you when it comes in."

"Which is when?" you ask.

"Three weeks, give or take a few days." When you say nothing, Nada goes on, "Ask for Captain Tanaka. He'll know what to do."

"Thanks, Nada," you say. "I knew you'd come through."

"Just go soon," Nada says. "It could leave any time in the next twelve hours."

After you hang up the phone, though, you're not sure what to do. The only way to get Saito on the *Okuri* is to deceive him. He's dead set against going to Japan. But you know you should get him there anyway, for his own good and yours.

On the other hand, trying to trick Saito could end up in disaster. Besides, do you really want to spend three weeks on a freighter?

*If you want to try to get Saito on the ship, turn to page 74.*

*u think you'd better try to go to Vancouver as agreed, turn to page 108.*

Two men burst out the door and immediately start choking on the smoke. "Check the stairs!" orders the voice you heard before. The men curse and cough as they run down the hall to the stairway.

The next two come out of the door together. You fling the metsubishi in their eyes, then let yourself drop from the ceiling and land on their shoulders. Straddling their heads between your knees, you scissor your legs together, knocking them out simultaneously. The three of you crash to the floor.

Disentangling yourself from the men, you get to your feet and rush into the room, your shuriken ready. You freeze, finding yourself face-to-face with the last man—the boss. He holds a gun in his hand and looks as if he's going to get a lot of pleasure out of pulling the trigger.

*Turn to page 113.*

You drag Saito up the gangway of the massive ship, then leave him behind on the main deck. Dodging through the galleries, you climb up deck after deck toward the bridge. You find Captain Tanaka, a white-haired man with a serene face, poring over some charts and puffing on a pipe. Breathlessly you explain who you are and what you need.

The captain chuckles. "I think we can accommodate you. But we'll have to keep you out of sight, just to be safe."

"Fine," you say. "There's one more thing. My companion thinks we're going to Vancouver, so—"

Just then Saito comes puffing onto the bridge. Apparently he's been making some inquiries of his own, because he's furious. The veins pound in his neck. "You tricked me!" he screams. "This ship's going to Yokohama, not Vancouver. Well, you can forget it. I'm not going! I'm getting off!"

"That may be perilous," says Captain Tanaka, who's been issuing instructions on an intercom while you argue. "The gangway has been taken up, and the tugboats are here. We're on our way."

You don't feel anything, but when you look out the porthole, you see that the docks appear to be moving. Saito pounds his head against the bulkhead.

Saito doesn't speak to you for a whole week. Captain Tanaka has set you up in an empty container. He's even had extra furniture and cots brought in for you.

*Turn to page 92.*

Holding the sword out in front of himself with both hands, Saito cries, "Hideomi, I dedicate my life to you!"

"Wait!" one of Hideomi's men cries. "Check the sword."

Saito hesitates, the sword poised in the air. He knows that form must be followed. Hideomi nods to his man, who comes forward to inspect the sword. If he does so, he'll see that it's a fake—it has a spring-operated retractable point.

The only way the fake suicide can proceed is if you pretend to attack Saito from behind, toppling the two of you over the edge. If you're lucky, Hideomi will believe you've plunged into the bay to your death.

On the other hand, you're not at all sure you want to make the bungy dive. Your backups should arrive soon. Maybe it's time for a change of plan.

*If you pretend to attack Saito,*
*turn to page 111.*

*If you let the man take the sword from Saito,*
*turn to page 45.*

"No thank you," you say to the man. You start to leave, but he grabs your arm. You jerk your elbow into his ribs, and while he's momentarily stunned, you place an arm across his chest, a leg behind his knees, and sweep him across your leg. He goes crashing to the ground, and you make a quick exit.

You stalk angrily up the street, looking for a bus stop. Finally you find one. Two transfers later, you're back at the BART station.

After you've crossed the bay into Oakland, you find it's not any easier to get to the Black Dragon. The neighborhood isn't much nicer, either.

The club is a crowded room full of the smell of cigarettes and Chinese food. Players crowd around green felt tables, shuffling what look like domino tiles. Some of the players have beepers attached to their belts. A lot of money seems to be changing hands.

*Turn to page 75.*

You take a chance and pull yourself back up to the roof, surprising the two yakuza. One of them immediately has a gun trained on you.

"Don't worry," you say, raising your hands. "We're on the same side. We both want to get Hideomi, right?"

Your words take a moment to register. Then the men laugh. "Right, we want to get Hideomi," one says. "We want to get him little weasels like you and Saito. Now, tell your friends down there to come up."

In a flash you realize you've made a terrible mistake. These are Hideomi's men. This whole thing is a setup—a test of Saito's loyalty. And you've just given him away.

You have one last hope. "It's a trap!" you call down to Keiku and Kurt. "Run!"

Something smashes down on the side of your head. Suddenly everything goes black.

When you regain consciousness, you feel as if you are swinging in a hammock. But you're terribly heavy. It is then that you realize you are wrapped in heavy chains. The yakuza are swinging you back and forth, about to heave you into the bay!

You wonder if Keiku and Kurt will be able to save Saito; you know they're too late to save you. As you go sailing through the air, you realize you'll have a hard time swimming in this outfit.

**The End**

You go upstairs to discuss your flight to Vancouver. "How are we going to pay for this?" you ask.

Saito twirls a rubber band around his finger. "I don't know," he says slowly. His manner frightens you. Not only doesn't he know, he no longer seems to care. "Do you have a credit card?"

"No," you answer slowly, "but my parents do. Maybe I can get their number and we can use it to buy the plane tickets."

You find your parents' credit card number and buy a pair of tickets for the next flight to Vancouver. You have no idea what you're going to do when you get there, but you'll worry about that later. You can call Nada from there and let her know your change in plans.

*Turn to page 115.*

"Saito, you've got to get out of town," you say. "I know we can find a place for you to hide. I have friends in Japan who can protect you."

Saito shakes his head slowly. "If you mean the Kurayama, forget it."

"What about Arthur Wujan, then? Won't he help you now?"

"I'm not running away," Saito says firmly. "What's the expression you Americans use—you have to make the bed you lie in?"

"Quit trying to be a hero!" you say in exasperation.

"I'm no hero!" he explodes. "I'm just a jerk who's got himself in a lot of trouble, and now for once in my life I'm going to face the consequences of my actions!"

"You don't have to die for making a few mistakes," you say softly.

Saito crumples up his napkin and throws it on the table. "It's time to go," he says, not looking at you.

Silently you pay the bill and walk out of the Happy Boy. "I'll give you a ride to the train station," Saito says."

"Never mind," you say. "I'll walk."

You're fuming as you head to the BART station. You decide that you're done with trying to help Saito. He's hopeless.

*Turn to page 76.*

With a bloodthirsty scream, you pretend you've broken your bonds. You grab Saito from behind, knocking the sword into the abyss. A quick jab to his kidneys disables him, then you heave him and yourself off the edge of the railing. You both scream in terror—this you're not faking.

Then there is silence. You spread your arms in a headfirst fall. You can see nothing but blackness around you. Everything seems to stop—your heart stops, your breathing stops, and yet you are plunging faster and faster toward the water. Hide-omi and his men can no longer see you.

Then you slow. You don't feel the bungy cord jerking on your ankles or anything, your fall just goes slower and slower until finally you stop altogether. You reach a bottom point and bounce back up, like a yo-yo on a string. It's the strangest feeling, as if the force of gravity has been powered down, then reversed.

As you bounce up and down at the end of your giant rubber band, you look over to see Saito doing the same thing. He looks at you and starts to laugh uncontrollably. You start laughing, too, so hard it hurts.

Finally the up-and-down boinging stops, and you are suspended in air, halfway between the bridge and the water. You can see the lights of a Coast Guard cutter below. You're glad you made that call. Now you just hope they figure out some way to get you off the bungy cord before all the blood in your body rushes to your head.

**The End**

The sailboat is sinking quickly, but luck seems to be with you today. Angel Island, which sits in the middle of the bay, is only a quarter mile away. You and Saito take off your shoes and abandon ship.

You swim hard for the island. Looking back, you see that the sailboat has sunk without a trace. The tanker still hides you from the yakuza. They'll have no idea what became of you.

By the time you and Saito pull yourselves ashore on Angel Island, the yakuza boat is nowhere to be seen. You take cover up in some trees just to be safe, but you figure they'll never look for you here. For now you can lie low and take a ferry back to the city later on.

*Turn to page 83.*

Suddenly there is a thunk on his neck, and he crumples to the ground. Saito emerges from behind him. "You!" he cries with shock.

Before you can answer, you feel intense heat at your back. Flames are leaping through the doorway—your smoke bomb must have ignited the old, dry wood of the building!

"We've got to get out of here!" you cry to Saito. "This place is a tinderbox!"

"The window!" Saito says, grabbing your arm.

But you resist. You're on the second floor. With your ninja skills you know you can survive the jump, but what about Saito? Maybe you'd be better off trying to get out with the crowd in the confusion downstairs.

*If you go to the window with Saito, turn to page 37.*

*If you tell him to come down the stairs, turn to page 66.*

As it turns out, Canadian customs solves the problem for you. You haven't been in Vancouver more than five minutes when the official inspecting your passports asks you to step into his office. "Your visa's expired," he says sternly to Saito.

You sit nervously in the office while the official disappears to make inquiries. When he returns, two police officers are with him. "Not only is your visa expired," he says, tight-lipped, "but you're wanted for arson in San Francisco."

The officers escort you onto a flight back to San Francisco. When you arrive, they turn you over to a federal marshal. You now have a charge of international flight added to your record.

A detective with the San Francisco police interrogates you and Saito in a closed room right there at the airport. You attempt to convince him that you're victims of the yakuza. Unfortunately, by trying to flee, your credibility has been shot. You can't deny that it was your smoke bomb that set off the fire.

The detective does give you some final words of advice. "You're going to need a good lawyer," he says.

**The End**

## ABOUT THE AUTHOR

**JAY LEIBOLD** was born in Denver, Colorado. He is the author of many books in the Choose Your Own Adventure series, including *Secret of the Ninja*, the sequel *Return of the Ninja*, *You Are a Millionaire*, *Revenge of the Russian Ghost*, and *Fight for Freedom*. He lives in San Francisco.

## ABOUT THE ILLUSTRATOR

**FRANK BOLLE** studied at Pratt Institute. He has worked as an illustrator for many national magazines and now creates and draws cartoons for magazines as well. He has also worked in advertising and children's educational materials and has drawn and collaborated on several newspaper comic strips, including *Annie* and *Winnie Winkle*. Most recently he has illustrated *The Case of the Silk King*, *Longhorn Territory*, *Track of the Bear*, *Master of Kung Fu*, *South Pole Sabotage*, *Return of the Ninja*, *You Are a Genius*, *Through the Black Hole*, *The Worst Day of Your Life*, *Master of Tae Kwon Do*, *The Cobra Connection*, *Hijacked!*, *Master of Karate*, and *Invaders From Within* in the Choose Your Own Adventure series. A native of Brooklyn Heights, New York, Mr. Bolle now lives and works in Westport, Connecticut.